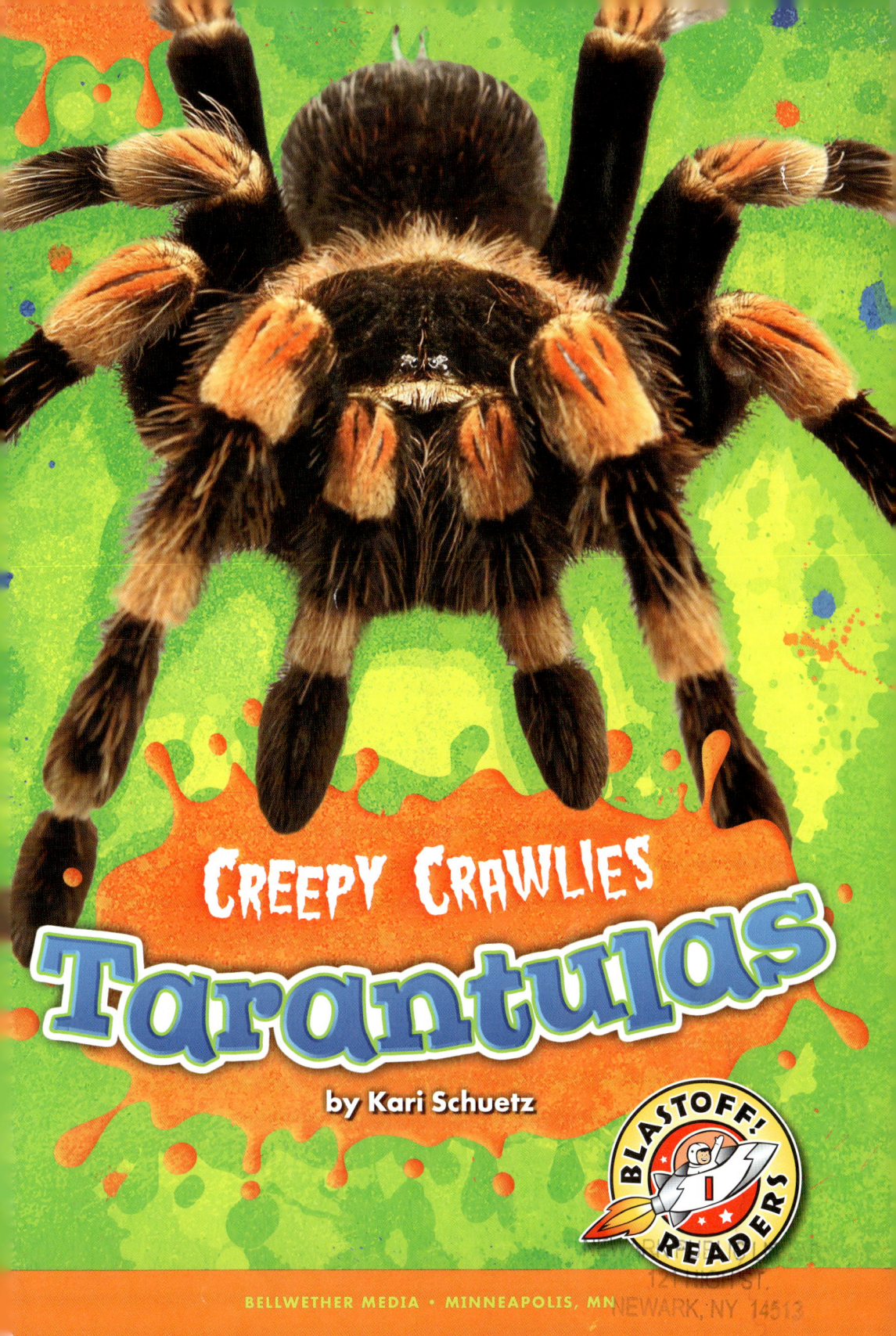

CREEPY CRAWLIES
Tarantulas

by Kari Schuetz

BLASTOFF! READERS

BELLWETHER MEDIA • MINNEAPOLIS, MN

Note to Librarians, Teachers, and Parents:

Blastoff! Readers are carefully developed by literacy experts and combine standards-based content with developmentally appropriate text.

Level 1 provides the most support through repetition of high-frequency words, light text, predictable sentence patterns, and strong visual support.

Level 2 offers early readers a bit more challenge through varied simple sentences, increased text load, and less repetition of high-frequency words.

Level 3 advances early-fluent readers toward fluency through increased text and concept load, less reliance on visuals, longer sentences, and more literary language.

Level 4 builds reading stamina by providing more text per page, increased use of punctuation, greater variation in sentence patterns, and increasingly challenging vocabulary.

Level 5 encourages children to move from "learning to read" to "reading to learn" by providing even more text, varied writing styles, and less familiar topics.

Whichever book is right for your reader, Blastoff! Readers are the perfect books to build confidence and encourage a love of reading that will last a lifetime!

This edition first published in 2016 by Bellwether Media, Inc.

No part of this publication may be reproduced in whole or in part without written permission of the publisher. For information regarding permission, write to Bellwether Media, Inc., Attention: Permissions Department, 5357 Penn Avenue South, Minneapolis, MN 55419.

Library of Congress Cataloging-in-Publication Data

Schuetz, Kari, author.
  Tarantulas / by Kari Schuetz.
     pages cm. – (Blastoff! Readers. Creepy Crawlies)
  Summary: "Developed by literacy experts for students in kindergarten through grade three, this book introduces tarantulas to young readers through leveled text and related photos"– Provided by publisher.
  Audience: Ages 5-8
  Audience: K to grade 3
  Includes bibliographical references and index.
  ISBN 978-1-62617-227-2 (hardcover: alk. paper)
  1. Tarantulas–Juvenile literature. I. Title.
  QL458.42.T5S38 2016
  595.4'4–dc23
                                           2015005965

Text copyright © 2016 by Bellwether Media, Inc. BLASTOFF! READERS and associated logos are trademarks and/or registered trademarks of Bellwether Media, Inc. SCHOLASTIC, CHILDREN'S PRESS, and associated logos are trademarks and/or registered trademarks of Scholastic Inc.

Printed in the United States of America, North Mankato, MN.

Table of Contents

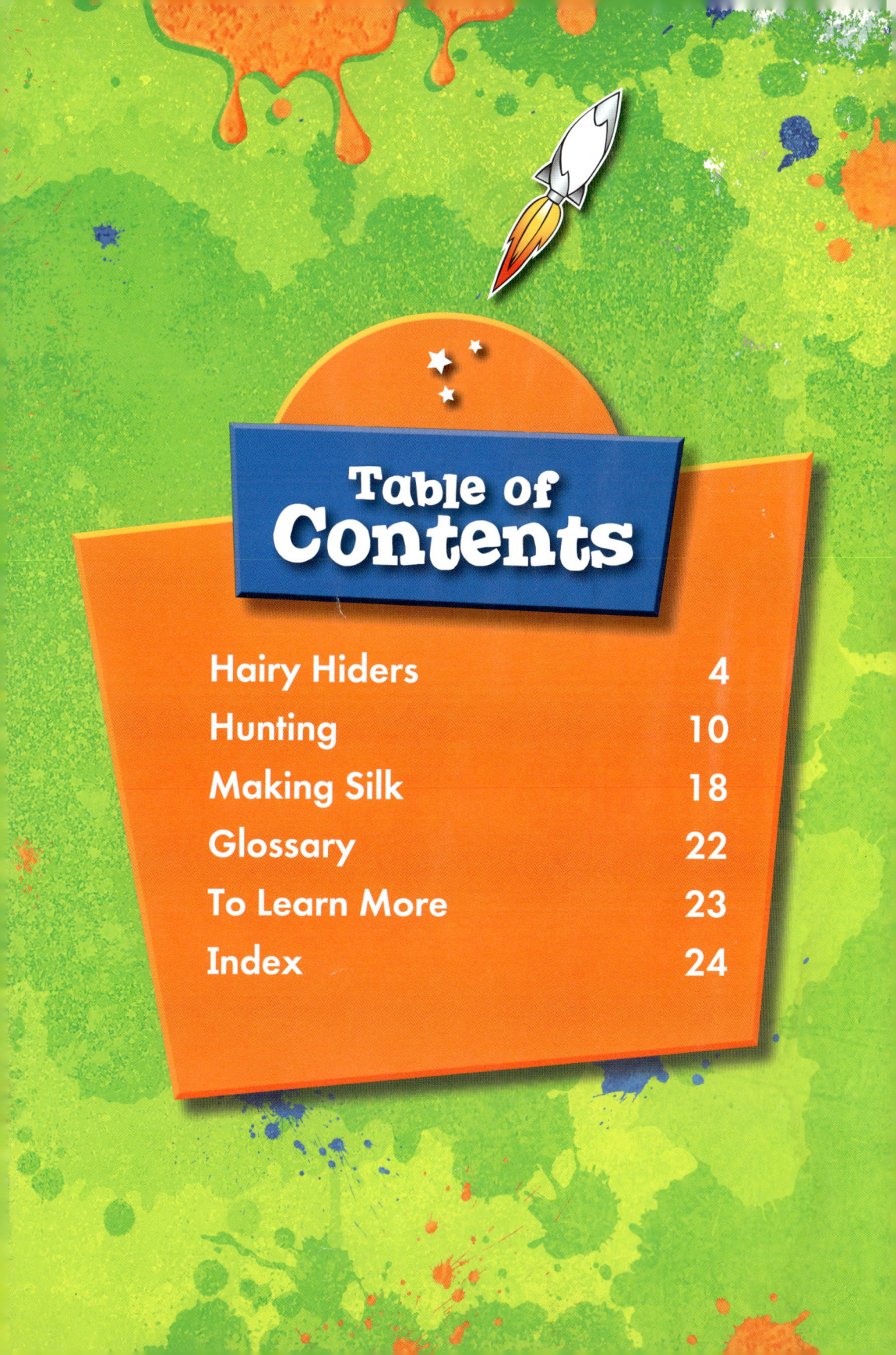

Hairy Hiders 4
Hunting 10
Making Silk 18
Glossary 22
To Learn More 23
Index 24

Hairy Hiders

Tarantulas are big **arachnids**. They have eight hairy legs!

These spiders live everywhere from deserts to **rain forests**.

They usually hide in **burrows** or under rocks.

Hunting

Tarantulas are hunters. They wait for **prey**.

They grab **insects** and other animals that come close.

Then their **fangs** bite with **venom**. Soon their prey stops moving.

The venom turns the prey into a liquid. Tarantulas slurp their meals.

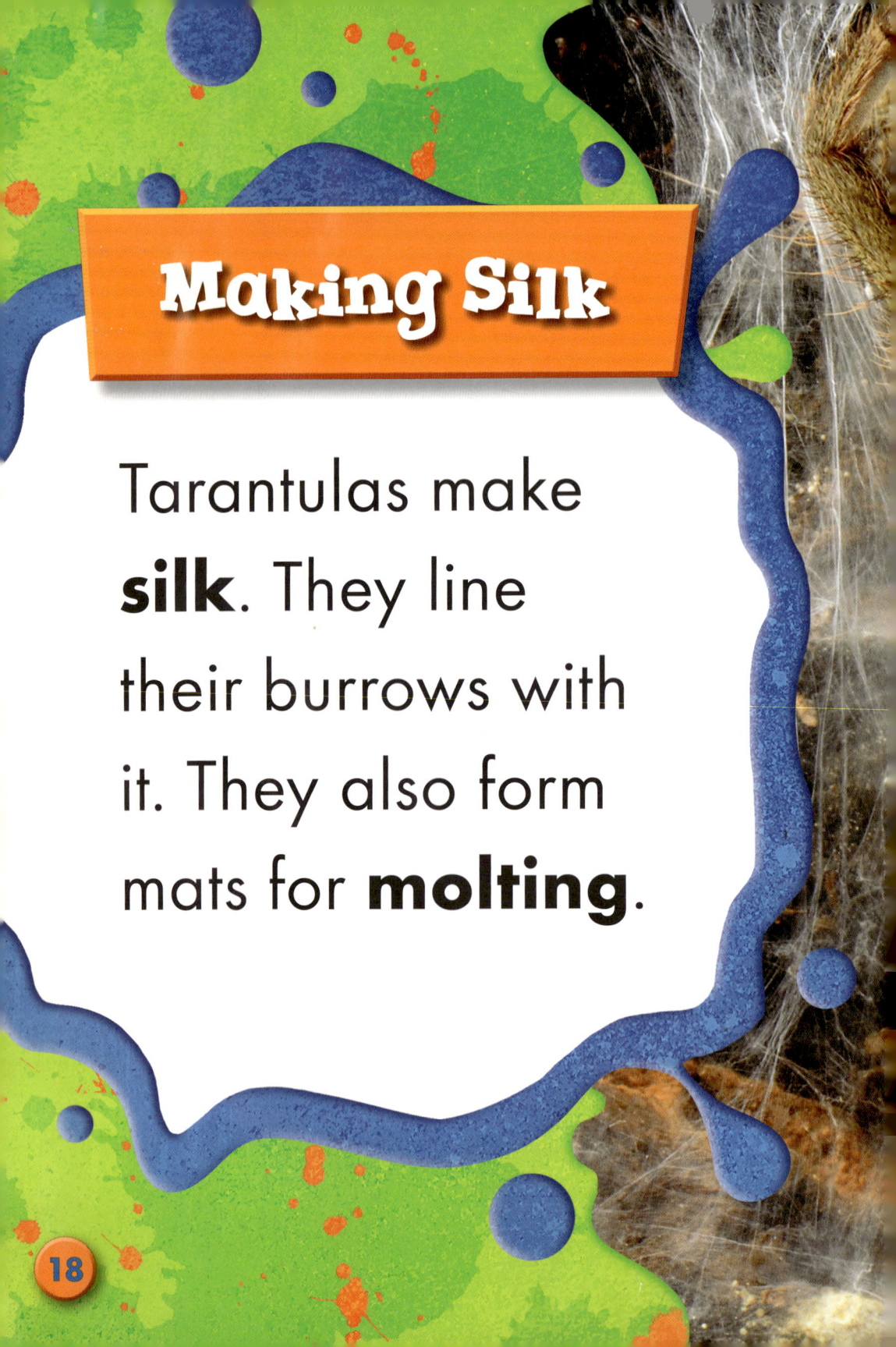

Making Silk

Tarantulas make **silk**. They line their burrows with it. They also form mats for **molting**.

They also cover their eggs in silk. This protects the eggs until babies **hatch**!

Glossary

arachnids—small animals with eight legs; an arachnid's body is divided into two parts.

burrows—holes or tunnels that some animals dig in the ground

fangs—sharp teeth; venom often flows through fangs.

hatch—to break out of an egg

insects—small animals with six legs and hard outer bodies; an insect's body is divided into three parts.

molting—shedding skin

prey—animals that are hunted by other animals for food

rain forests—warm forests that receive a lot of rain

silk—a strong, soft material

venom—a poison

To Learn More

AT THE LIBRARY

Borgert-Spaniol, Megan. *Spiders*. Minneapolis, Minn.: Bellwether Media, 2014.

Ganeri, Anita. *Tarantula*. Chicago, Ill.: Heinemann Library, 2011.

Hughes, Catherine D. *Little Kids First Big Book of Bugs*. Washington, D.C.: National Geographic Society, 2014.

ON THE WEB

Learning more about tarantulas is as easy as 1, 2, 3.

1. Go to www.factsurfer.com.

2. Enter "tarantulas" into the search box.

3. Click the "Surf" button and you will see a list of related web sites.

With factsurfer.com, finding more information is just a click away.

Index

arachnids, 4
babies, 20
bite, 14
burrows, 8, 18
deserts, 6
eggs, 20
fangs, 14
grab, 12
hairy, 4
hatch, 20
hide, 8
hunters, 10
insects, 12
legs, 4
liquid, 16
mats, 18
molting, 18

prey, 10, 14, 16
protects, 20
rain forests, 6
rocks, 8
silk, 18, 20
slurp, 16
spiders, 6
venom, 14, 16

The images in this book are reproduced through the courtesy of: Mirek Kijewski, front cover; Cathy Keifer, p. 5; Minden Pictures/ SuperStock, p. 7; Ch'ien Lee/ Minden Pictures/ Corbis, p. 9; skydie, p. 11 (top); Guinter Fernandes Costa, p. 11 (bottom); Dirk Ercken, p. 13; P. Wegner/ Arco Images GmbH/ Glow Images, pp. 15, 17; Lighthouse/ UIG/ Age Fotostock, p. 19; Ryan M. Bolton, p. 21.